THE UNEXPURGATED ADVENTURES OF SHERLOCK HOLMES

BOOK 6

THE MAN WITH THE HAIRY FACE

by NP Sercombe

The un-edited manuscript originally entitled
The Man With The Twisted Lip written by
Dr. John Watson and Sir Arthur Conan Doyle

Illustrations by Emily Snape

Published by EVA BOOKS 2019 – c/o Harry King Films Limited
1&2 The Barn
West Stoke Road
Lavant
n/r Chichester
West Sussex PO18 9AA

Copyright © NP Sercombe 2020

The rights of Nicholas Sercombe to be identified as the author of this work have been asserted in accordance with the Copyright, Designs and Patents Act 1988.

A CIP catalogue record for this book is available from the British Library.

ISBN 978-1-9996961-5-3 (Hardback)

Book layout & Cover design by Clare Brayshaw.

Cover illustration by Emily Snape.

Set in Bruce Old Style.

Prepared and printed by: York Publishing Services Ltd
64 Hallfield Road, Layerthorpe, York YO31 7ZQ

Tel: 01904 431213

Website: www.yps-publishing.co.uk

THE UNEXPURGATED ADVENTURES OF

SHERLOCK HOLMES

Books in the Series:

Nicholas Sercombe is a writer and producer for film and television. He has been lucky enough to work in comedy for most of the Holocene period with some of the greatest performers and writers. He is most comfortable when reading Conan Doyle and even happier when re-writing these extraordinarily entertaining stories by Dr. John Watson.

Emily Snape is a coffee addicted, London based illustrator, who's work can be found internationally in books, magazines, on the web, television and even buses.

She studied at Central Saint Martins, Bristol and Kingston and is rarely found without a pencil in her hand. She loves sketching in the streets of London and thinks life is too short for matching socks.

For hirsute people who enjoy laughing

The Man With The Hairy Face

(*published in The Strand in December 1891 as*
THE MAN WITH THE TWISTED LIP
by Dr. Watson and Arthur Conan Doyle)

Isa Whitney, the brother of the late Elias Whitney, D.D., Principal of the Theological College of St. George's, was Scottish. He was also a right pain-in-the-arse because he was much addicted to opium. The habit grew upon him, as I understand, from some foolish freak when he was at college; for having read De Quincey's dreams and sensations, he had drenched his tobacco with laudanum in an attempt to produce the same effects. What an idiot! He found, of course, as so many more have done, that the practice is easier to attain than to get rid of, and for many years he continued to be a slave to the drug, an object of mingled horror and pity to his friends and relatives. I can see him now, with yellow, pasty face, drooping lids and pin-pointed pupils, all huddled in a chair, the wreck and ruin of a noble man. As I just mentioned: this man was an idiot.

One evening – it was in June '89 – there came a knock upon the door of my consulting room door in Queensbury Place, South Kensington, about the hour when a man thinks that his day's work is finished and glances at the clock. I groaned to myself, for I was weary, but sat up in my chair and bade: "Come!" The door was opened by my nephew and novice practice manager, William, but before he could utter a word there were some quick steps upon the walnut parquet behind him. The door flew open, and a lady, clad in some dark-coloured stuff with a black veil, entered the room at high speed. I stood up, walked around my desk to greet her and she came to an abrupt halt in front of me.

'You will excuse my calling so late...' she began but then, suddenly, she lost her self-control. She ran forward, threw her arms about my neck, and sobbed upon my shoulder. 'Oh! I am in such trouble, John!' she cried; 'I do so want a little help!'

Behind her back William's face lit up, his eyebrows raised in speculative and lurid anticipation because she was a pretty young thing, now quivering all over me and wetting my shirt front with her tears. He was grinning like a Frenchman's mistress and gave me a wink and double thumbs-up; in my defence I flicked him a winsome *deux doigts d'Agincourt*. He retreated from the room, closing the door with a silent laugh. How the youth of the day could have such disrespect for their elders was a mystery to me – I was never brought up in such a liberal way – because this was after I had rebuked him for wasting my money on an under-the-counter acquisition of the "Manstopper" revolver, which was so powerful it made the weapon of no use whatsoever.[*]

'Oh!' I said, standing back half a step and lifting her veil. 'It is you, Kate! Kate Whitney! How you startled me. All I could see was a woman.'

---

[*]   see *The Oranges of Death!*

'Well, *I am* a woman!' she blustered, now putting herself back into order.

'I am sorry, Kate. I was taken by surprise. I had not an idea who you were when you came in.'

'Please excuse me, John, for bursting in on you like this. I am all of a flutter. I didn't know what to do, so I came straight to you.'

This was a very unusual situation for me. Folk who were in grief tended to come to my friend, Mr. Sherlock Holmes, like fleas to a kennel yard, not to yours truly.

'Nonsense, Kate. It is very sweet of you to come at any time. Now, you must have some wine and water, and sit here comfortably and tell me all about it. Or would you rather take your clothes off and lie down on the couch?'

Her eyes popped searchlight and her jaw dropped anchor until the twinkle in my eye betrayed my tease. She laughed and threw her arms around me again, then pushed me away gently in mock scorn.

'Oh John! For a moment I took you seriously! You haven't changed a bit!' she mocked.

I laughed with her but really, I had meant what I said. I had always fancied Kate, right from childhood. She was small and blonde and lovely, a little box of fireworks, always pinging about the place, never standing still, and always teasing us boys and running off. Even as adolescents, when the onset of hormones removed our innocence, I had never had a chance to get my hands on her, not even to give her a peck on the cheek, before I was whisked off to the army. Anyway, I lowered my voice to a seriously professional tone and went for a double dose of John Watson humour.

'Kate, you know that I was attempting to lift your mood a little, if I was able, but I see that you are in great distress. Here…' And I moved behind a comfortable armchair and held it for her in invitation. She relaxed and looked at me sympathetically with her beautiful blue eyes. She smiled and lowered herself gracefully down towards the seat but just before her peachy landed on the cushion I whispered: 'but clothes off first!' And this time I received a proper punch in the gut! Then, she sat down. Slightly winded, I waddled over to the desk and sat back down opposite her, just as she started off in earnest.

'It isn't just you, John, as a friend, from whom I seek advice. I want your advice as a doctor and your help too. It is about Isa.'

'I am not surprised,' I replied.

'He has not been home for two days,' said she. 'I am frightened about him.'

It was not the first time that she had spoken to me of her husband's ongoing opium addiction trouble, to me as a doctor as well as a friend and old school companion. Previously, I had soothed and comforted her by such words as I could find but, this time, he had gone one step further – by disappearing. I asked her if it was it possible that I could bring him back to her and if she knew where her husband was?

It seemed that she had the surest information that of late he had, when the fit was on him, made for of an opium den in the furthest east of the City. Hitherto his orgies had always been confined to one day, and he had come back, twitching and shattered, in the evening. But now the spell had been upon him eight and forty hours, and he lay there, doubtless, among the dregs

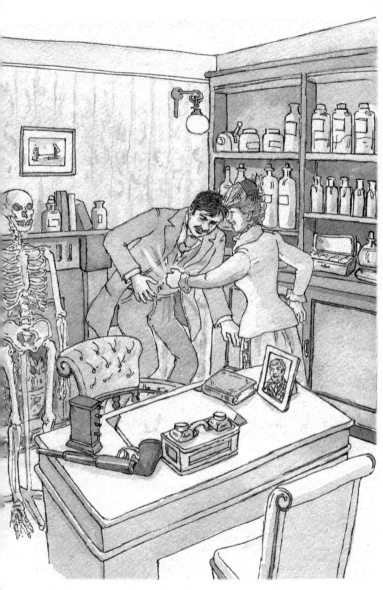

wasn't difficult to work out that Kate was married to a Scotsman.

of the docks, breathing in the poison of sleeping off the effects. There he was to be found, she was sure of it, at the 'Bar of Gold' in Upper Swandam Lane. But what was she to do? How could she, a young and timid woman, make her way into such a place, and pluck her husband out from among the ruffians who surrounded him?

There was the case and, of course, there was only one way out of it. Might I not escort her to this place? But, then, maybe there was another option: of making the exploration on my own, the second thought of why she should come at all? I was, after all, Isa Whitney's medical adviser, and as such I had influence over him. I could manage the task better if I were alone. She had me cornered there, and I had to admit it to myself. What is more, I couldn't afford to lose the faith of my few clients, especially opium addicts with money. I promised her on my word that I would find him and send him home in a cab within two hours if he were indeed at the address which she had given me. And so, in only ten minutes, I had left my nice warm consulting rooms behind me as the *knight errant* and was speeding eastwards in a hansom on a strange errand as it seemed to me at the time. Only the future could show how strange it would be and whether Kate would show her gratitude in the way that my lewd imagination suggested.

There was no great difficulty in the first stage of my adventure. Upper Swandam Lane, a vile alley lurking behind the high wharves which line the north side of the river to the east of London Bridge. Between a slop shop and a gin shop, approached by a steep flight of steps leading down to a black gap, like the mouth of a cave. I found the den of which I was in search. Ordering my cab to wait, I passed down the steps, worn hollow in the centre by the ceaseless tread of drunken feet, and by the light of the flickering oil lamp above the door. I found the latch and made my way into a low room, thick and heavy with the brown opium smoke, and terraced with wooden berths, like the forecastle of an emigrant ship.

Through the gloom one could dimly catch a glimpse of bodies lying in strange fantastic poses, bowed shoulders, bent knees, heads thrown back and chins pointing upwards, with here and there a dark, lacklustre eye turned upon the newcomer. Out of the black shadows there glimmered little red circles of light, now bright, now faint, as the burning poison waxed or waned in the bowels of the metal pipes. The most lay silent, but some muttered to themselves, and others talked together in a strange, low, monotonous voice, their conversations coming in gushes, and the suddenly tailing off into silence, each mumbling out his own thoughts, and paying little heed to the words of his neighbour. At the furthest end was a small brazier of burning charcoal, beside which on a three-legged wooden stool there sat a tall, thin old man, with his jaw resting upon his two fists, and his elbows upon his knees, staring into the fire.

As I entered, a sallow Malay attendant had hurried up with a pipe for me and a supply of the drug, beckoning me to an empty berth.

'Thank you. I have not come to stay,' said I. 'There is a friend of mine here, Mr. Isa Whitney, and I wish to speak to him. Have you seen him?' The chink looked at me wide-eyed, as if he was stuck in a vacuum. 'Now come along… He speaks in a very strange way. Very hard to understand. No? I'll give you a clue: he's Scottish.'

There was a movement and an exclamation from my right, and peering through the gloom, I saw Whitney, pale, haggard and unkempt, staring out at me.

'Oh, mair Good! It's Wotsin!' said he. He was in a pitiable state of reaction, with every nerve in a twitter. 'Ah say Wotsin, whit's tha' hooer?'

'Nearly eleven.'

'O' whit day?'

'Of Friday, 19th June.'

'Guid heavens! Ah thought 'twas Wensday. 'Tis Wensday! How come dai yi'll want tai frighten a chap fooer?' He sank his face on to his arm and began to sob in a high treble key.

'I tell you that it is Friday, you Scotch madman! Your wife has been waiting two days for you. You should be ashamed of yourself.'

'So, ah am, laddie! But you hae yer mind mixed, Wotsin, fur ah ha' bin heeyur but a few hooers, theree pipes, fooer pipes – I furgit ha' menny. But ah'll goo hoom wit' yer. Ah woodn'a frightin Kate. Puir wee Kate! Gimme yer haun! Hulp me up! Ha' yoo a cab?'

'Why yes, my lord,' I said in a mockingly deferential tone. 'Your carriage awaits you, oh noble one.' He may have been fugged out of his tiny one, but he recognised sarcasm surely enough and the caveman within him made a guest appearance – he curled his lip in a snarl, shook his first and shot me a glare that could have come straight from the Gorbals.

'Poot a sock in it, Doctor! Ooer ah'll batter yer wun! Ah'm in enough jobby as is! Naw, I mist owe sumthin' heeyur. Will'ya feend aat what ah owe, Wotsin. Ah'm awff colour. Ah ken doo nuthin' for meself.' And before I could say "pay for it yourself, you Scotch kipper!" he slumped down onto the floor and retched violently. What a git!

I turned on my heel, somewhat abashed by his tone, and had trouser-warming thought; if he was out of his mind most of the time, incapable of doing anything for himself, how I might liaise with Kate for some long-overdue intimacies. I walked off down a narrow passage between the double-row of sleepers, holding my breath to keep out the vile, stupefying fumes of the drug and embraced these fine thoughts about Kate and I locked together in a rhythmic clinch. These were colourful images of a lustful embrace, one that was pent-up because I had visited it many times in my life: Kate, all soft and naked and voluptuous; me, all young and virile and thrusting... Goodness! Why was I imagining such lurid thoughts in a dreadful pace like this?! There could only be one reason, dear reader, and so I started counting back the days since the last time I had the intimate pleasure a woman. As you might expect, I found it to be unreconcilable, hence the state of my frustrated imagination. It was simply ages ago! So, there lay the diagnosis and I was in the perfect position to prescribe the medicine – I would send myself off to Mother Kelly's as soon as I was finished here!

Eventually, I shook my head back to reality and started to look about for the manager. As I passed the tall man who sat by the brazier, I felt a sudden pluck at my coat, and a low voice whispered: 'Walk past me, and then look back at me.' The words fell quite distinctly upon my ear. I glanced down. They could not have come from the old man at my side, and yet he sat now as absorbed as ever, very thin, very wrinkled, bent with age, an opium pipe dangling down between his knees, as though it had dropped in sheer lassitude from his fingers. I took two steps forward and looked back. It took all my self-control to prevent me from breaking out into a cry of astonishment. He had turned his back so that none could see him but I. His form had filled out, his wrinkles were gone, the dull eyes had regained their fire, and there, sitting by the fire, and grinning at my surprise, was none other than Sherlock Holmes! He made a slight motion to me to approach him, and instantly, as he turned his face half round to the company once more, subsided into a doddering, loose-lipped senility.

'Holmes!' I whispered. 'What on Earth are you doing here? You never mentioned your intention to patronize this den over breakfast this morning.'

'Nor did you, Doctor! Now, keep your voice as low as you can – I have excellent ears and very fine hearing. If you would have the great kindness to get rid of that Scottish friend of yours, I should be exceedingly glad to have a little talk to you.'

'He is not a friend, Holmes, he is a patient.'

'A patient? Then, get rid of that loud-mouthed Jimmy!'

'All right, I am in the process of doing so. I have a cab outside.'

'Pray, put him in it. You may trust him to get home. Just look at the state of him. He is too desolated to get into any mischief. Then, I shall meet you outside in five minutes.'

'I shall do that immediately, Holmes.' And I marched back towards Mr. Isa Whitney who I could see in the distance lolling about the place, just like a round-bottomed toy, completely out of his mind.

'And Watson...' Holmes hissed after me, 'if I was you, I would recommend you send a note with him for the cabman to hand to his wife relating the tale of how you overcame great danger to valiantly save her husband. In this way, you may ingratiate yourself adequately for her to invite you into her *boudoir* to foist your years of pent-up desires upon her. Ha!'

I stopped dead in my tracks and swung round. 'HOW?!' I cried, 'DID YOU KNOW WHAT I WAS THINKING?'

But all Sherlock Holmes did was turn away and shrink his body back down once more to that of the crippled opium victim, all huddled and hunched, his face hidden away from public scrutiny. For a moment I was bewildered about how the great detective could read my mind. Just...how?! I suppose, I reasoned, we were young men of energetic years – he, twenty-nine, and me, thirty – who lived together in mental harmony and, therefore, understood one another's needs. Maybe I mentioned Kate and Isa at some time in the past and now his great brain percolated that information and he could make a deduction and then surprise me with such a bold declaration? But then, unfortunately, I was distracted by a tap on my arm: it was the manager, who indicated to me to be silent after my shouting and to behave myself, or else.... I acknowledged his petulant request and grabbed my Scottish Jimmy by the scruff of his neck. In a few minutes I had written my note, paid his bill and confined him to a cab. Once he had been safely despatched, I found myself thinking that my mission was practically accomplished; and for the rest, I could not wish anything better than to be associated with my friend in one of those singular adventures which were the normal condition of his existence. It was not long before a decrepit figure had emerged from the opium den, and I was walking down the street with Sherlock Holmes. For two streets he shuffled along with a bent back and an uncertain foot. Then, glancing quickly around, he straightened himself out and burst into a hearty fit of laughter.

'I suppose, Watson,' said he, 'that you imagine that I have added opium-smoking to cocaine use and all the other little weaknesses on which you have favoured me with your medical views.'

'I was certainly surprised to find you there.'

'But not more so than I to find you.'

'I came to find a client, one my very few patients.'

'You cannot afford to lose any of that rare species, Doctor!'

'Oh ha-ha, Holmes. I'll have you know that my nephew and I have recruited a fine platoon of patients on my clinical books. They may all have "special needs" but they pay for my professional consultation. But you still haven't answered my question.'

'I came to find an enemy.'

'An enemy? Would that be like James Moriarty? My only encounter with Professor Moriarty convinced me that you two are sworn enemies.'*

'No. Opium dens are not his line of business, Watson. The Professor prefers to hunt prey in the

---

* see *The Oranges of Death!*

When Isa was on an opium binge he was a right pain in the Isa!

lucrative surroundings of high finance, sometimes in the City of London. Sometimes he dabbles in more personal extortion, but only with royalty, and the rich and famous, but I hear that he is moving up in the underworld and into the dark art of government blackmail. It is only there that the responsibility of the misuse of public money may be deferred until it is too late for recovery or the blame re-distributed amongst nameless officials so that no single person is culpable.'

'That is scandalous, Holmes,' I scowled, 'but makes for a very sensible strategy. I have to say, this Professor fellow seems to be going places.'

'Indeed so, Watson. Indeed so...'

'Do you think he would have a vacancy for a young accomplice, of the medical persuasion, somebody like me, for instance?'

'No, Watson, you are far too honest. Anyway, that's enough of Moriarty. I am in the midst of a very remarkable inquiry and I had hoped to find a clue in the incoherent ramblings of the opium sots, as I have done before now. By the way, had I been recognised in that den my life would not have been worth an hour's purchase, for I have used it before now for my own purposes, and the rascally Lascar who runs it has sworn vengeance upon me. There is a trap-door at the back of that building, near the corner of Paul's Wharf, which could tell me some strange tales of what has passed through it upon moonless nights.'

'What? You do not mean bodies?'

'Aye, bodies, Watson. We would be rich men if we had a thousand pounds for every poor devil who had been done to death in that den. It is the vilest murder-trap on the whole river-side, and I fear that the object of my client's commission, a certain Neville St. Claire, has entered it never to leave it more. But my trap should be here...' He put her two forefingers between his teeth and whistled shrilly, a signal which was answered by a similar from the distance, followed shortly by the rattle of wheels and the clink of horse's hoofs.

'Now, Watson,' said Holmes, as a tall dog cart dashed up through the gloom, throwing out two golden tunnels of yellow light from its side-lanterns, 'you'll come with me, won't you?'

'If I can be of use.'

'Good. Then I have no need for this driver here. I don't suppose you have half a crown about your person to pay him off?'

'No. I just gave every last farthing I had to that Lascar.'

Holmes patted his pockets, but they were empty, as usual. 'Me as well. This will be tricky, Watson, for my driver here is a very rough sort.'

The dog cart drew up beside us. Holmes leaned in towards me and whispered: 'He will not take kindly to our impecunious state. We shall have to scare him off. Follow my lead...' Holmes tapped the side of his nose surreptitiously.

Mischief! The chase was on. I prepared myself...

The driver mock-doffed his cap to us. He was a mighty burly looking cove, rough as granite, with a shifty look about him. He was introduced to me as Bobby McKeowan, which confirmed he was an Irish navvy with a second income. Holmes flashed his eyes at me. We were under starter's orders.

'Thank you, Doctor, for joining me,' he announced loudly, to ensure reception by the navvy. 'A trusty comrade is always of use. And a chronicler still more so. My rooms at The Cedars is a double-bedded one. Nice and comfy. You must join me.'

'I could make excellent use of a new story, Holmes, but I am not willing to sleep with you to acquire it.'

A glimpse of trepidation flitted across McKeowan's eyes.

'Oh, please, Doctor! That never worried you before. The Cedars is only seven miles in that direction.' The great detective pointed to the east as he clambered up on to the bench next to McKeowan, who now looked distinctly uncomfortable. 'I am staying at Mr. St. Clair's house is in Lee, in Kent, while I conduct the inquiry and we shall make a fine couple to comfort Mrs. St. Clair.'

'Ah! Then his wife will be there. I shall be safe.'

'Don't play hard to get, Doctor. I won't bite...too hard. Now jump up and sit next to me.'

A glimpse of anger flitted across McKeowan's eyes.

I jumped up next to the navvy and made sure my leg touched onto his. McKeowan snapped his head round to look at me, all wide-eyed and outraged. His eyes dropped down to our legs touching and when I made no effort to move, his eyes lifted back up to mine. I looked into his eyes and smiled.

'This is very cosy, Mister McKeowan, but could be even cosier.' I wriggled in closer. McKeowan flinched, like I was an electric eel, but he didn't make a run for it. Yet. Holmes flashed his eyes at me.

'Very!' said Holmes, and he shifted closer on his other side, sandwiching between us.

'If you cupp-ala queer ones wanna be on your tods, give me my dues and I'm off!'

Holmes ignored him and leaned across our driver to get to me. 'No, McKeowan, we need a driver because seven miles of jigging around on this contraption in the middle of the night will be highly stimulating.'

Holmes was, of course, referring to the involuntary increase in blood-flow to the *glans penis* when the male body is subjected to a constant up and down movement on the posterior.

'I remember you have a rather vulgar expression in the army, Watson? Now, what was it? Carriage...? Carriage... something?'

'Cock!'

'Don't mind if I do, Doctor!'

That did it! McKeowan jumped to his feet and belted out his foulest homosexual expletives! Then, he jumped backwards, scrambled around behind us, clambered furiously over the wooden bulwark and, finally, leapt off the cart. I'll swear that he hit the ground running! He disappeared far off into the gloom, still shouting at us. Holmes and I were triumphant! He even cried after him, still playing up.

'Goodnight sweetie! I'll be back tomorrow at about eleven!' Once he was out of earshot, we both collapsed and laughed and laughed and laughed, probably the most since Miss Sutherland thrashed the living daylights out of Mr. James Windibanks!*

---

* see *The Case of the Randy Stepfather.*

Eventually, Holmes wiped his eyes and picked up the reins. He flicked the horse with the whip, and we trotted away through the endless succession of sombre and deserted streets, still laughing spasmodically at the fond memory of such an idyllic reaction to our prank. We went flying across a broad balustraded bridge, with the murky river below flowing sluggishly, and beyond us lay another broad wilderness of bricks and mortar, its silence broken only by the heavy, regular footfall of the policeman, or the songs and shouts of some belated party revellers. A dull wrack was drifting slowly across the sky, and a star of two twinkled dimly here and there through the rifts of the clouds. Holmes drove in silence – I think that we had worn ourselves out with our mirth earlier on – and he had his head sunk down upon his breast, and the air of a man who is lost in thought, whilst I sat beside him curious to learn what this new quest might be which seemed to tax his powers so sorely, and yet afraid to break in upon the current of his thoughts. We had driven several miles and were beginning to get to the fringe of the belt of suburban villas, when he shook himself, shrugged his shoulders, and lit up his pipe – pup! pup! – with the air of a man who has satisfied himself that he is acting for the best.

'You have a grand gift of silence, Watson,' said he, pup-pup! 'It makes you quite invaluable as – pup! – a companion. 'Upon my word, it is a great thing for me to have someone to talk to, for my own thoughts are not – pup! – over-pleasant. I was wondering what is should say to the dear little woman tonight when she meets me at the – pup! – door.'

'You forget that I know nothing about it. I, too, have a little woman situation who I feel sorry for.'

'But you have returned your charge to her safe and sound. I go back to my employer with empty hands.'

'When you say "employer," is this a hint that you are charging for your services?'

'Don't be – pup! – impertinent, Watson. Now, I shall just have time to tell you about my – pup! – case before we get to the – pup! – town of Lee.'

'But could you please do it, Holmes, without all that infernal pipe on the go. All that pup-pup-pupping is driving me mad.'

'All right, Doctor...' Holmes pocketed the pipe. 'My case seems absurdly simple, and yet, somehow, I can get nothing to go upon. There's plenty of thread, no doubt, but I can't get the end of it in my hands. Now, I'll state the facts clearly and concisely to you, Watson, and maybe you may see a spark of light when all around me is clouded in darkness.'

'I shall try my best to shine a beam of sunlight through your cumulonimbus.'

He threw me a glance of cynical indifference.

'Sorry... Proceed! Proceed!'

'Some years ago – to be definite, in May 1884 – there came to Lee a gentleman, Neville St. Clair by name, who appeared to have plenty of money. He took a large villa, laid out the grounds very nicely, and lived generally in good style. By degrees he made friends in the neighbourhood, and in 1887 he married the daughter of a local brewer, by whom he now has two children. He had no occupation but was interested in several companies and went into town as a rule in the morning, returning by the 5.14 from Cannon Street every night. Mr. St. Clair is now thirty-seven years of age, is a man of temperate habits, a good husband, a very affectionate father, and a man who is popular with all who know him. I may add that his whole debts at the present moment, as far as we have been able to ascertain, amount to £220 and 10 shillings whilst he has £2,110 standing to his credit at the Capital and Counties Bank. There is no reason, therefore, to think that money troubles have been weighing upon his mind.

'Last Monday Mr. Neville St. Clair went into town rather earlier than usual, remarking before he started that he had two important commissions to perform, and that he would bring his little boy home a box of bricks.'

'Lucky boy!'

'Shut up, Watson. Now, by the merest chance, his wife received a telegram upon the same Monday, very shortly after his departure, to the effect that a small parcel of considerable value which she had been expecting was waiting for her at the offices of the Aberdeen Shipping Company. Now, if you are well up on your London, you will know that the office of the company is in Fresno Street, which branches out of Upper Swandam Lane, where you found me tonight. Mrs. St. Clair had her lunch, started for the City, did some shopping, proceeded to the company's office, got her packet, and found herself at exactly 4.35 walking through Swandam Lane on her way back to the station. Have you followed me so far?'

'It is as clear as a goldfish bowl, Holmes.'

'IF you remember, Watson, Monday was an exceedingly hot day, and Mrs. St. Clair walked slowly, glancing about in the hope of seeing a cab, as she did not like the neighbourhood in which she found herself. While she was walking in this way down Swandam Lane, she suddenly heard an ejaculation....'

Now Holmes had my full attention!

'... or cry...'

Oh...

'... and was struck cold to see her husband looking down at her and, as it seemed to her, beckoning to her from a second-floor window. The window was open, and she distinctly saw his face, which was agitated. He waved his hands frantically to her, and then vanished from the window so suddenly that it seemed to her that he had been plucked back by some irresistible force from behind. One singular point which struck her quick feminine eye was that although he wore some dark coat, such as he had started to town in that morning, he had on neither collar nor necktie.'

'Holmes – he sounds like a rum sort of fellow who was having a little distraction from the missus, wouldn't you say?'

'No! Not necessarily, Watson... convinced that something was amiss with him, she rushed down the steps – for the house was none other than the opium den in which your patient was patronising tonight – and running through the front room she attempted to ascend the stairs which led to the first floor. At the foot of the stairs, however, she met this Lascar scoundrel, who we have both met, who thrust her back and, aided by a Dane, who acts as assistant there, pushed her out into the street. Filled with the most maddening doubts and fears, she rushed down the lane and, by rare good fortune, met in Fresno Street a number of constables with an inspector, all on their way to their beat. The inspector and two men accompanied her back, and in spite of the continued resistance of the proprietor, they made their way to the room in which Mr. St. Clair had last been seen. There was no sign of him there. In fact, in the whole of that floor there was no one to be found save a crippled wretch of a hideous aspect, who, it seems, made his home there. Both he and the Lascar stoutly swore that no one else had been front room during the afternoon. So determined was their denial that the inspector was staggered and had almost come to believe that Mrs. St. Clair has been deluded when, with a cry, she sprang at a small deal box which lay upon the table and tore the lid from it. Out there fell a cascade of children's bricks. It was the toy he had promised to bring home.

'This discovery, and the evident confusion which the cripple showed, made the inspector realise that the matter was serious. The rooms were carefully examined, and the results all pointed to an abominable crime. The front room was plainly furnished as a sitting room and led into a small bedroom, which looked out upon the back of one of the wharves. Between the wharf and the bedroom window is a narrow strip, which is dry at low tide but is covered at high tide with at least four and half feet of water. The bedroom window was a broad one and opened from below. On examination traces of blood were to be seen upon the windowsill, and several scattered drops were visible upon the wooden floor of the bedroom. Thrust away behind a curtain in the front room were all the clothes of Mr. Neville St. Clair, with the exception of his coat. His boots, his socks, his hat, and his watch – all were there. There were no signs of violence upon any of these garments, and there were no other traces of Mr. Neville St. Clair. Out of the window he must apparently have gone for no other exit could be discovered, and the ominous bloodstains upon the sill gave little promise that he could save himself by swimming, for the tide was at its very highest at the moment of the tragedy.

'And now as to the villains who seemed to be immediately implicated in the matter. The Lascar was known to be a man of the vilest antecedents, but as, by Mrs. St. Clair's story, he was known to have been at the foot of the stair within a very few seconds of her husband's appearance at the window, he could hardly have been more than an accessory to the crime. His defence was one of absolute ignorance, and he protested that he had no knowledge as to the doings of Hugh Boone, his lodger, and that he could not account in any way for the presence of the missing gentleman's clothes.

'So much for the Lascar manager. Now for the sinister cripple who lives upon the second floor of the opium den, and who was certainly the last human being whose eyes rested upon Neville St. Clair. His name is Hugh Boone, and his hirsute face is one which is familiar to every man who goes much to the City. He is a professional beggar, though in order to avoid the police regulations he appears to be a small trader in wax vestas.'

'Matches?'

'Indeed, Watson. Some little distance down Threadneedle Street, upon the left-hand side, there is, you may have noticed, a small angle in the wall. Here it is that this creature takes his daily seat, cross-legged with his tiny stock of matches on his lap, and as he is a piteous spectacle a small rain of charity descends into the greasy leather cap which lies upon the pavement beside him. I have watched the fellow more than once before ever I thought of making his professional acquaintance, and I have been surprised at the harvest which he has reaped in a short time. His appearance, you see, is so remarkable that no one can pass him without observing him.'

'My word, Holmes, what is this mark of esteem?'

'He has a shock of hair that hides his pale face completely.'

'What do you mean by "completely?"'

'His entire head is covered in hair. The only feature one can only just make out is the twinkle of his vividly penetrating eyes when caught in direct sunlight.'

'Oh, don't be ridiculous, Holmes! Nobody can have hair around their eyes! It is a physical impossibility. *Homo sapiens* does not have hair follicles in the epidermis north of the zygomatic bone or within the infraorbital margin or on the eyelid or forehead below the superciliary arch. That is a biological fact and the end of it.'

'This man possesses such follicles. And each hair grows to the same length. It is, therefore, forming a perfectly round ball of hair around his head. He has a similar in appearance to an *allium giganteum* in the herbaceous border of a fine English garden.'

'He looks like the allium flower?' Holmes nodded acknowledgement. 'That is preposterous!' I continued. 'And I suppose he is as ginger as Mr. Jabez Wilson?*

'How did you know?'

'Oh Holmes, please... You cannot expect me to fall for such a blatant fib. Do you forget that I have trained as a medic?'

---

* see *The Mysterious Case of Mr. Gingernuts*

'It is true.'

'So, this chap has a crippled body with a ball of ginger hair sitting upon his shoulders?'

'A ball of hair is all that any person may see of him.'

'Poppeycock!'

'Perhaps you would like to suggest a wager upon your opinion, Doctor?'

'Certainly. Five pounds will make up for your insult to my integrity.' This was a bold wager considering I had less than one pound to my name at that particular moment in my life, but I can remember my training and know my facts, and no la-di-da detective was going to change those.

'Take my word it is true, Watson, so make it five guineas.'

We shook hands. 'Anything you like, Holmes. Ha!'

'There is more to this man than just hair. What marks this man out from the common crowd of mendicants is his wit, for he is ever ready with a reply to any piece of chaff which may be thrown at him by passers-by. This is the man whom we now learn to have been the last man to see the gentleman of whom we are in quest.'

'It is just his wit that makes him stand out, not the fact that he looks like a ginger dandelion?'

'That is so, Watson,' he replied, gravely.

'Holmes, I do not believe this story! Regardless of his hairy face and his razor wit, how could this Hugh Boone cripple chappy have overcome a man, single-handedly, in the prime of his life, such as Mr. St. Clair?'

'He is a cripple in a sense that he walks with a limp; but, in other respects, he appears to be a powerful and well-nurtured man. Surely your medical experience would tell you, Watson, that weakness in one limb is often compensated for by exceptional strength in others.'

'Sometimes that is so, but even then, these facts, at best, sound fanciful. Pray, continue your narrative, Holmes.'

'Why thank you, Doctor! Mrs. St. Clair had fainted at the sight of the blood upon the window, and she was escorted home in a cab by the police, as her presence could be on no help to them in their investigation. Inspector Barton, who had charge of the case, made a very careful examination of the premises, but without finding anything which threw any light upon the matter. One mistake had been made in not arresting Boone instantly, as he was allowed some few minutes during which he might have communicated with his friend the Lascar, but this fault was soon remedied, and he was seized and searched, without anything being found which could incriminate him. There were, it is true, some bloodstains upon his right shirt-sleeve, but he pointed to his ring finger, which had been cut near the nail, and explained that the bleeding came from there, adding that he had been to the window not long before, and that the stains which had been observed there came doubtless from the same source. He denied strenuously having ever seen Mr. Neville St. Clair, and swore that the presence of the clothes in his room was as much a mystery to him as to the police. As to Mrs. St. Clair's assertion, that she had actually seen her husband at the window, he declared that she must have been either mad or dreaming. He was removed, loudly protesting, to the police station, while the inspector remained upon the premises in the hope that the ebbing tide might afford some fresh clue.

'And it did, though they hardly found upon the mudbank what they had feared to find. It was Neville St. Clair's coat, and not Neville St. Clair, which lay uncovered as the tide receded. And what do you think they found in the pockets?'

'Crabs?'

'No, I don't think you will guess. Every pocket stuffed with pennies and halfpennies – four hundred and twenty-one pennies, and two hundred and seventy halfpennies. It was no wonder it had not been swept away by the tide. But a human body is a different matter. There is a fierce eddy between the wharf and the house. It seemed likely enough that the weighted coat had remained when the stripped body had been sucked away.'

'Now that sounds feasible, what with the tide coming in and going out, but...'

'Don't interrupt, Watson!'

'...but surely, Holmes, if all the other clothes were found in the room, would the body be dressed in the coat alone?'

'I fine point made, Doctor, but no. The facts might be met speciously enough. Suppose that this man Boone had thrust Neville St. Clair through the window, there is no human eye which could have seen the deed. What would he do then? It would of course instantly strike him that he must get rid of the tell-tale garment. He would seize the coat then, and be in the act of throwing it out, when it would occur to him that it would swim and not sink. He has little time, for he had heard the scuffle downstairs when the wife tried to force her way up, and perhaps he has already heard from his Lascar confederate that the police are hurrying up the street. There is not an instant to be lost. He rushes to some secret hoard, where he has accumulated the fruits of his beggary, and he stuffs all the coins upon which he can lay his hands into the pockets to make sure of the coat's sinking. He throws it out and would have done the same with the other garments, had not he heard the rush of steps below, and only just had time to close the window when the police appeared.'

'That sounds more like it.'

'Well, we will take it as a working hypothesis for want of a better. Boone, as I have told you, was arrested and taken to the station, but it could not be shown that there had ever before been anything against him. He had for years been known as a professional beggar, but his life appeared to have been a very quiet and innocent one. There the matter stands at present, and the questions which have to be solved, what Neville St. Clair was doing in the opium den, what happened to him when there, where he is now, and what Hugh Boone had to do with his disappearance, are all as a far from solution as ever. I confess that I cannot recall any case within my experience which looked at first glance so simple, and yet which presented such difficulties.'

Whilst Sherlock Holmes had been detailing this singular series of events we had been whirling through the outskirts of the great town until the last straggling houses had been left behind, and we rattled along with a country hedge upon either side of us. Just as he finished, however, we drove through two scattered villages, where a few lights glimmered in the windows.

'We are on the outskirts of Lee,' said my companion. 'We have driven six and a half miles, touched on three English counties and I have an acute case of carriage cock.'

I looked over at the great detective's crotch; even in the feint glow of moonlight I noticed an extreme strain on the cloth of his trousers.

'I have to confess, it is the same with me, Holmes.'

'Let me have a look...'. Holmes looked over and studied my crotch. He nodded. 'It is the same,' he confirmed.

He pulled on the reins and brought the dog-cart to a halt. 'Do you see that light among the trees?' he said. 'That is The Cedars, and beside that lamp sits Mrs. Neville St. Clair, a woman who is extremely anxious. I suggest we dismount until our conditions have subsided.'

'I agree. We wouldn't wish to offend the poor lady.'

'There is that consideration, but I must tell you that Mrs. St. Clair is a woman who is in charge of her own destiny,' said Holmes, the meaning of which I wouldn't find out until much later on. 'It is only this singular event that has thrown her off course.'

We climbed down carefully from the cart's wooden bench; almost gingerly... Even so, oh it was a painful experience! We waddled around in circles, like parrots, whilst our muscles gradually re-adjusted themselves to a normal state of comfort. We stretched and we yawned. It gave me a chance to quiz Holmes a little more about the matter in hand.

'Why are you not conducting the case from Baker Street, Holmes?' I asked.

'Because there are many inquiries which must be made out here.'

'Really?'

'Yes. And Mrs. St. Clair has most kindly put some rooms at my disposal. You may be rest assured that she will have nothing but a welcome for my friend and colleague, even you, Doctor!'

'Oh ha-ruddy-ha, Holmes.'

'But I hate to return to her, Watson, when I have no news of her husband. Now, are you comfortable?'

'Yes, thank you, Holmes. I am as limp as an Archbishop's handshake at a schoolgirls swimming gala.'

'Ha! Oh, very good, Watson! You should join forces with Mr. Hugh Boone. Let us proceed to The Cedars there. I have little doubt that Mrs. St. Clair caught the clink of our horse's feet.'

We clambered back up onto the dog cart. Our pony trotted the last hundred yards or so through the gates to The Cedars. With a completely unnecessarily dramatic "whoa, there whoa!" from Holmes, we pulled up in front of a large villa, which stood within its own grounds. A stable boy ran out of the side of the house to the horse's head. This time we sprang down from the bench all-nimble, fresh as daisies. I followed Holmes up the small, winding gravel drive which led to the house. As we approached the door flew open, and a little blonde woman stood in the opening, clad in some sort of light *mousseline-de-soie* – I should know, dear adventure-enthusiast, ladies' lingerie being a pet fetish of mine – with a touch of fluffy pink chiffon at her neck and her wrists. She had the appearance of an exquisite fairy about to climb into her woodland bed but prevented from doing so by our arrival. She stood with her figure outlined against the flood of light, one hand upon the door, one half raised in eagerness, her body slightly bent, her head and face protruded with eager eyes and parted lips. She had an air of vulnerability that all men find alluring, but I found her to be more than that – I found her to be *extremely* attractive and an unexpected arrow of desire punctured my heart, whistled through the other side and ricocheted off my perineum and instantly revived my carriage cock! Even so, I was mesmerized, because, all of a sudden, she rushed forwards, her gorgeous, delicate, bare feet patting on the wooden floor, and embraced Sherlock Holmes, but not like an acquaintance, or even a sibling, and certainly not like a client, but more like a long lost lover, with kisses and trembling and real passion. My imagination stopped in its tracks, and I must have blanched, because now I found myself to be the unexpected guest, this unanticipated affection being a little awkward to witness. Embarrassed, I looked away behind me at the boy walking the cart away to the stables and by the time I had turned back she had retreated back to the threshold, thank goodness, resuming her position and bearing of before.

'Well?' she cried. 'Well?!' And then, seeing that there were two of us, she gave a most attractive cry of hope...until Holmes introduced me to her. After a polite handshake she sank into a groan as she saw that my companion shook his head and shrugged his shoulders.

'Is there any good news, Sherlock?'

'None.'

'No bad news, Sherlock?'

'No.'

'Thank God for that! You must be weary, for you have had a long day.'

'And a long, uncomfortable journey.'

'Carriage cock?'

We both nodded.

'You poor chaps. Please, come in.'

We followed Mrs. St. Clair through the hallway. She walked daintily, and Holmes filled her in with his news. 'My friend here, Dr. Watson, has been of most vital use to me in several of my cases, and a lucky chance has made it possible for me to bring him out and associate him with this investigation.'

'I am delighted to see you here and for your support,' said she. 'You will, I am sure, forgive anything which has come so suddenly upon us.'

'My dear madam,' said I, 'I am an old campaigner, and if I were not, I can very well see that no apology is needed. If I can be of any assistance, either to you or to my friend here, I shall indeed be happy.'

'Now, Mr. Sherlock Holmes,' said the lady as we entered a well-lit dining room, upon the table of which a cold supper had been laid out. 'I should very much like to ask you one or two plain questions, to which I beg that you will give a plain answer.'

'Certainly, madam,' said he, in passing, as he sat down at the table his eyes scanning the fare and settling upon a very fat bird.

'Do not trouble about my feelings. I am not hysterical, not given to fainting. I simply wish to hear your real, real opinion.'

'Upon what point?' said he again, this time wrenching the entire leg off of a turkey carcase.

'In your heart of hearts, do you think that Neville is alive?'

Sherlock Holmes seemed to be embarrassed by the question, whilst he chomped into the dark flesh in a quest to quench his appetite. 'Frankly now!' she repeated, standing upon one leg, upon the rug, and looking keenly down at him, as he leaned back in a mediocre-quality commercial reproduction of a Sheraton chair, the turkey grease glistening on his chin.

'Frankly, then, madam, I do not.'

'You think that he is dead?'

'I do.' Chomp!

'Murdered?'

'I don't say that. Perhaps.' Chomp! Chomp!

'And on what day did he meet his death?'

'On Monday.'

'Then perhaps, Mr. Holmes, you will be good enough to explain how it is that I have received this letter from him today?'

Sherlock Holmes sprang out of the chair as if he had sat on something red hot.

'THIS IS REMARKABLE!' he roared, whilst waving the massacred turkey leg in the air.

'Yes, today.' She stood smiling, holding up a little slip of paper in the air.

'May I see it?'

'Certainly.'

He stood up and snatched it from her in his eagerness.

'Easy, tiger…' she quipped.

Tiger? Did I imagine that to be over-familiar? Well, frankly, yes … In his excitement, Holmes ignored her anyway and smoothed the paper out on the table. He leaned over it and studied the paper in great detail not even noticing the turkey juices dripping onto the handwriting. I was embarrassed by his behaviour. I looked at Mrs. St. Clair and noticed she thought the same. I couldn't help covering the incident for my friend.

'My apologies,' I said to her, 'his habitual good manners have been altered by exposure today to a heady atmosphere of opium in that Swandam Lane sewer.'

'Fear not for me, Doctor,' she whispered, touching my arm lightly with her hand, which made me tingle all over, 'I have witnessed this type of bad mood many times from my husband.' Then, she leaned against me to gain a closer observation of the great detective in action, that light denier of *mousseline-de-soie* allowing the warmth of her body to seep into mine. This had red-blooded consequences! Goodness, did she know what she was doing to me?

Whilst I tried to control myself, Holmes drew over the lamp and examined the paper intently. I was gazing at it over his shoulder and Mrs. St. Clair was bent over me to gain a view, so all three of us were almost on top of one another. My goodness, this was a most unusual *ménage* made more tricky for me by our hostess wafting warm, perfumed breaths into my ear.

Mrs. St. Clair was the hostess-with-the-mostest.

Holmes told us that the envelope was a very coarse one, and was stamped with the Gravesend postmark, and with the date that very day, or rather of the day before, for it was considerably after midnight.

'Coarse handwriting!' murmured Holmes. 'Surely this is not your husband's? It is nearly as illegible as Watson's.'

'No, but the enclosure is.'

'I perceive also that whoever addressed the envelope had to go and inquire as to the address.'

'How can you tell that?'

'The name, you see, is in perfectly black ink, which has dried itself. The rest is of the greyish colour, which shows that blotting-paper has been used. If it had been written straight off, and then blotted, none would be of a deep black shade. This man has written the name, and there has been a pause before he wrote the address, which can only mean that he was not familiar with it. it is, of course, a trifle, but there is nothing so important as trifles.'

'Hear, hear Holmes. I love a sherry trifle!'

Holmes stood up abruptly. Mrs. St. Clair jumped back away from me, disconnecting the *ménage* entirely. Holmes inclined his head towards me and glared; I looked to my right and found Mrs. St. Clair doing the same, making it worst by placing her hands on her hips.

'I am sorry...'

Eventually, Holmes turned back to the envelope and extracted a paper from it. 'Let us now see the letter! Ha! There has been an enclosure here!'

'Yes, there was a ring. His signet ring.'

'And you are sure that this is your husband's hand?'

'One of his hands.'

'One? The left or his right?'

'Neither and nor.'

Holmes and I exchanged glances of modest astonishment, which our hostess noticed.

'Fear not, my valiant detectives, it is his hand when he wrote hurriedly. It is very unlike his usual writing, and yet I recognise it.'

Holmes selected a chicken drumstick in the style of a well-seasoned finger buffet aficionado and sat back down in his chair. With the other hand he held the letter and read to us: '"Dearest, do not be frightened. All will come well. There is a huge error which it may take some time to rectify. Wait in patience." And it is signed Neville. It is written in pencil upon a flyleaf of a book, octavo size, no watermark. Posted today in Gravesend by a man with a dirty thumb. Ha! And the flap has been gummed, if I am not very much in error, by a person chewing tobacco.'

'Yeuch!' squealed Mrs. St. Clair, puckering her alembicated features at Sherlock Holmes.

'My apologies' said Holmes, lifting the juicy drumstick from his lips, placing it on a plate and wiping the herb-ridden fat from his mouth with a folded napkin.

'No, I mean the tobacco chewing.'

'Oh, I see…'. He picked up the chicken again. 'And you have no doubt that it is your husband's hand, madam?' he said, waving it around like a baton.

'YES!'

'Then he might have called to you?'

'He might, I suppose...'

'He only, as I understand, gave an inarticulate cry?'

'Yes.'

'A call for help, you thought?'

'Yes. And he waved his hands.'

'But it might have been a cry of surprise? Astonishment at the unexpected sight of you might cause him to throw up his hands?'

'It is possible, but Neville isn't prone to over-excitement.'

'And you thought he was pulled back?'

'He disappeared so suddenly.'

'Hmm! He had probably just heard Watson's appalling trifle joke. You did not see anyone else in the room?'

'No, but that horrible man confessed to having been there, and the Lascar was at the foot of the stairs.'

'Quite so. Your husband, as far as you could see, had his ordinary clothes on?'

Yes, but without his collar and tie. I distinctly saw his bare throat.'

'Had he ever spoken of Swandam Lane?'

'Never.'

'Had he ever shown any signs of having taken opium?'

'Never.'

'Thank you, Mrs. St. Clair. Those are the principal points about which I wished to be absolutely clear. We shall now have a little supper and then retire, for we may have a very busy day tomorrow.'

'Then I shall leave you to it. I bid you goodnight, gentlemen.' Our hostess disappeared from the room.

We settled into our cold supper with a vengeance. Afterwards, we made our way upstairs to find that a comfortable double-bedded room had been placed at our disposal. I was into pyjamas quickly and then between the sheets, for I was weary after my night of adventure. Sherlock Holmes was a man, however, who when he had an unsolved problem upon his mind would go for days, and even for a week, without rest, turning it over, rearranging his facts, looking at it from every point of view, until he had either fathomed it, or convinced himself that his data were insufficient. It was soon evident to me that he was now preparing for an all-night sitting. He took off his coat and waistcoat, put on a large blue dressing-gown, and then wandered about the room collecting pillows from his bed, and cushions from the sofa and armchairs. With these he constructed a sort of Eastern divan, upon which he perched himself cross-legged, with an ounce of shag tobacco and a box of matches laid out in front of him. In the dim light of the lamp I saw him sitting there, pup-pup-pupping on an old briar pipe between his lips, his eyes fixed vacantly upon the corner of the ceiling, the blue smoke curling up from him, silent, motionless, with the light shining upon his strong-set aquiline features. So he sat as I dropped off to sleep, and I was restless throughout the night. I dreamed and, as is so often the case when the mind is working fast, that people involved in my most recent events featured within the episodes. Firstly, there was the driveway of The Cedars; there was the stable boy; and there was

Sherlock Holmes. Then, in the second dream, there was Mrs. St. Clair. One minute she was standing by the front door looking so exquisitely gorgeous in her night attire that I confess to feeling embarrassed by my attraction to her, even within the secure confines of my own mind. In the third dream there she was again, this time on the temporary divan in my room, making passionate love to Sherlock Holmes! Just as I was taking stock of our client astride the consulting detective, gyrating her hips like a Billericay Beauty on overtime, I felt her eyes suddenly set upon me – whilst still *in flagrante,* I might add – and then bore into mine.

"Come, Doctor!" she gasped huskily, beckoning me with her forefinger. "Three is never a crowd – it is twice the pleasure.'

Had my imagination gone wild? I felt an unerring compulsion to obey her and before I could make any sense of things, I had abandoned my bed and stood in front of them both. I knew it was wrong – what was I doing there? – but I stepped out of my jim-jams, thus crossing the Rubicon of day-to-day decency set out in our conformist Society. My mind was buzzing! My heart was racing! I presented my credentials to Mrs. St. Clair. She smiled. So did Holmes! Each extended a hand to me and I was drawn onto the temporary divan of contemplation and welcomed with open arms. The next thing I knew, we had become wild animals in the throes of ecstasy – our hostess, Mrs. St. Claire, my dear friend, Sherlock Holmes and your humble reporter all together as one, writhing naked upon the cushions (now, the temporary divan of lust). All five senses buzzed with the heady intenseness of sensuality: the sight of young, healthy bodies conjoined in eroticism;

the smell of perfumed secretions saturating my olfactory with its sweet aromas; the frisson of epidermal contact tingling my nerve endings with a spangle; the kneading of human fingers on succulent young flesh heightening my chances of, one day, maybe, playing the piano. Oh, I was in heaven! But suddenly, through this hazy crescendo of passion, an intense feeling surged up through my loins. I found myself thrusting into Mrs. St. Clair with intense desire and vigour. My mind was boiling over, the sweat pouring off my naked body, the sap shooting up inside me, and, oh! here it was at last, I was com...

'STOP THAT, WATSON! STOP IT, I SAY'

Suddenly, it was the ceiling! An unfamiliar ceiling, but suddenly one that confirmed I was wide awake. I was being shaken on both shoulders by a fully clothed Sherlock Holmes, his bemused face restoring me to my senses. He inclined his head and smiled smugly at me.

'It looks to me like you experiencing a dream,' said he, 'of the Mount Vesuvius variety, am I not correct, Doctor?'

And, of course, he was. Or, was he? Surely, it must have been a dream?! But, was it? I sat up in bed and took in my surroundings; I had to gather my wits together to try and establish whether it had all been in my mind and please, Lord, not in real life; I just couldn't fathom whether I been hornswoggled by my own imagination? I applied the same methods as the great detective would do himself. First of all, I noted that Sherlock Holmes was fully dressed when I awoke, so how could that be so if it had been reality? Then, I checked for any sign of our hostess in the room, and there was none, so how could she have departed so quickly without me knowing? But then, just assurance gave me confidence, I double-checked the cushion arrangement of the temporary divan and, to my dismay, I recognized it as precisely the same layout we had used in the *ménage à trois* to make "the human catapult" work for Mrs. St. Clair. Oh, my goodness, maybe it was not a dream after all! I had been conscious all the time. Or had I? I found myself with options between what may have been my memory and what could have been created in my imagination. I studied Sherlock Holmes, who had descended back down onto the cushions with the pipe between his lips, but there was no answer to my dilemma there. He spied me and gave one determined pup! and smoke curled upwards.

'Are you game for a morning pup! drive, Watson?' enquired Holmes, pup! pup!

'Certainly, Holmes,' I said. I could not help but notice that he was in almost exactly the same position as when had I dozed off. Had the two of us made love to Mrs. St Clair? Or had it all been a fantasy? I pinched myself hard to stop thinking about it.

'Then pup! dress yourself and we shall go. No one is pup! stirring yet, but I know where the pup! pup! stable-boy sleeps, and we shall soon have the trap out.' Pup! He chuckled to himself as he spoke, his eyes twinkled, and he seemed a different man to the sombre thinker of the previous night – just like any chap who has unwound the knot of lust that lies tied up in our loins. Hmm!

As I dressed, I glanced at my watch. It was only twenty-five minutes past four! It was no wonder that no one was stirring yet. The house was as quiet as an actuaries' orgy. No! Dammit! I had to stop thinking

-42-

about things, especially the *ménage*! I pinched myself harder and had only just finished dressing when Holmes returned with the news that boy was putting in the horse (whatever that meant I dreaded to think)!

'I want to test a little theory of mine,' said he, pulling on his boots. 'I think, Watson, that you are now standing in the presence of one of the most absolute fools in Europe. I deserve to be kicked from here to Charing Cross. But I think that I have the key to the affair now.'

'And where is it?' I asked, smiling.

'In the bathroom,' he answered. 'Oh, yes, I am not joking,' he continued, seeing my look of incredulity. 'I have just been there, and I have taken it out, and I have got it in this Gladstone bag. Come on, my boy, and we shall see whether it will not fit the lock.'

We made our way downstairs as quickly as possible and out into the bright morning sunshine. As we marched briskly down the driveway, I looked over my shoulder back at the house, only to see Mrs. St. Clair staring out at us. She noticed me and caught my eye with a gentle wave of her fingers. I waved back, very nervously and cut short, because I'll swear she was naked! Oh, my goodness, now what was I supposed to think?!

In the road stood our horse and trap, with the half-clad stable boy waiting at the head. We both sprang in, and away we dashed down the London road. A few country carts were driving around, bearing in vegetables to the metropolis, but the lines of villas on either side were as silent and lifeless as some city in a dream. Was it a dream last night? Maybe? Maybe not...? No! Stop it!

'It has been in some points a singular case,' said Holmes, flicking the horse on into a gallop. 'I confess that I have been as blind as a mole, but it is better to learn wisdom late, than never to learn at all.'

In town, the earliest risers were just beginning to look sleepily from their windows as we drove through the streets of the Surrey side. Passing down the Waterloo Bridge Road we crossed over the river and, dashing up Wellington Street, wheeled sharply to the right and found ourselves in Bow Street. Sherlock Holmes pulled on the reins to bring us to halt outside the police station. He was well known to the Force, and two constables at the door saluted him. One of them held the horse's head while the other led us in.

'Who is on duty?'

'Inspector Dog and Bone, sir.'

'Inspector Dogandbone? There is no such person at this station.'

'Ha! Only kidding, mister Holmes! Coo, not much gets past you, does it, eh?'

'No, it does not. It must have been a long night, sergeant. Now, who is on duty, please?' Holmes was getting tetchy, drumming his fingers.

'No, really, it is sir. Well, it is a nickname, but it is a new one!'

'Sergeant! Just because a new telegraph machine known as a 'telephone' has been installed yesterday, in the supervising inspector's office, between the globe and bookshelf, there is no reason for a new nick...'

'Mr. Holmes! How did you know about the telephone installation? It is supposed to be a secret.'

'Ah, Bradstreet, how are you?' said Holmes, walking forwards with his hand outstretched. A stout official had come down the stone-flagged passage dressed in a peaked cap and frogged jacket. 'I wish to have a word with you, Bradstreet.'

'Certainly, Mr. Holmes. Step into my room here. But how about the telephone?'

'Elementary, dear Inspector,' said he as they walked into the adjacent office with Holmes pointing up to the ceiling cornice where two wires had been tacked underneath and then drilled through the wall two yards from the corner. Bradstreet looked up and sighed in resignation. He knew when was beaten.

It was a small office-like room, with a huge ledger upon the table and the new telephone device projecting from the wall. This was an absolute sensation! A *real* telephone! The very latest machine that allows one person to speak to another in a completely different neighbourhood. It was on the front cover of every fashionable magazine and the talk of the salons, the pubs and the racecourses around the land.

The inspector sat down at his desk and gestured Sherlock Holmes to sit down in the single chair opposite.

'What can I do for you, Mr. Holmes?'

'I called about that beggar-man, Boone – the one who was charged with being concerned in the disappearance of Mr. Neville St. Clair, of Lee.'

'Yes. He was brought up and remanded for further enquiries.'

'So, I heard. You have him here?'

'Yes. In the cells?'

'Is he quiet?'

'Oh, he gives no trouble. But he is a dirty scoundrel.'

'Dirty?'

'Yes, it is all we can do to make him wash his hands, and we cannot even see his face because it is covered completely in orange hair. When we try to part it, he becomes angry and aggressive. None of my lads can get near him. Well, when once his case has been settled, he will have a regular prison bath and an enforced encounter with the barber-in-residence. He won't like that, it being a farthing for the pleasure and a penny for a cut with styling, but I think, if you saw him, you would agree with me that he needs it.'

'I should like to see him very much.'

'Would you?'

'Yes, I would.'

'Well tell that medical mate of yours to stop meddling with my telephone device over there!'

I looked over to see what all the shouting was about only to see the great detective wheeled around in his chair to catch sight of me with the u-shaped part of the device clamped to my ear and my forefinger tapping upon the sticky-uppy thing protruding from its cradle. All of a sudden, I heard a sweet female voice:

"Hello. What district and number do you require, please?"

'Put that down, Watson! It is not a toy.'

'Oi! Put that down!' shouted Bradstreet.

"Hello? Is there anybody there? What number do you require, please?"

'Doesn't she sound lovely, chaps?' And then she repeated her questions to me.

'Hello? Yes, I am here. Doctor Watson at your service, my dear. What is your name?'

"Er, thank you... erm, I don't know what to say ... Do you require a line, please?"

The inspector's face reddened. 'That is police property!' he shouted, and then jumped up from his chair. Just as he rounded his desk and was striding towards me the u-shaped lady sounded more earnest.

"Do you require a line, please, sir? What number do you require, please?"

'Doctor – may I suggest you speak into the tulip-shaped part of the telephone device?'

'Right-o, Holmes.'

I moved closer to the sticky-up bit and said, rather suavely: 'Good morning to you, my dear! My name is John. Now, I just wondered if you are at a loose end this evening?'

Suddenly, Bradstreet was upon me. He snatched the u-shaped thing from my hand and veered off but my days on the rugger field stood me well. *"Ooh, thank you, Mr. John, but, erm... actually, I don't have anything plans..."* I grabbed him about his rather portly midriff and swivelled him around, reaching out to retrieve the thing back from him. I think that I called him a Thug and a Vandal and a number of other things at the same time, but soon victory was mine and I had possession of the device.

"Do you require a line, please?"

'What sort of line?' I asked it. 'A railway line?'

Amazingly, I could meet girls on this new-fangled telephone machin

Bradstreet hadn't given in. 'Give me that!' he shouted. He grabbed me by the collar and clamped his hand around mine in a bid to crush my fingers and release the device.

'Keep off the railway line, my dear...' I shouted, as I was fighting off the stout inspector, 'There's a train coming!' But then Holmes inserted himself in between us and suddenly I found myself back into a *ménage à trois* with the great detective, the shock of which made me resign and go limp – Holmes is a very strong man – and Bradstreet relaxed his grip too. The u-shaped thingy was taken from my hand and reunited with the rest of the telephone device and, unfortunately, the sweet lady's voice was no more.

'That's enough, gentlemen...'

Bradstreet glared at me as he re-aligned his clothing back to respectability and then glanced at Holmes. 'Come this way, gentlemen. You can leave your bag here.'

'No, I shall take it,' said Holmes. 'I think that we shall all find its contents useful.'

'If you must but come this way, if you please.' He led us down a passage, opened a barred door, passed down a winding stair, and brought us to a whitewashed corridor with a line of doors on each side.

'The third on the right is his,' said the inspector. 'Here it is!' He quietly shot back a panel in the upper part of the door and glanced through.

'He is asleep,' said he. 'You can see him very well.'

We both put our eyes to the grating. The prisoner lay on an iron bed. By studying the position of his torso, I assumed that he had his face towards us, but

I could not be entirely sure because his head was one great bauble of ginger hair! He was in a very deep sleep, breathing slowly and heavily. He was a middle-sized man, coarsely clad as became his calling, with a coloured shirt protruding through the rent in his tattered coat. He was, as the inspector had said, extremely dirty, but the grime which was visible to us only covered his hands and part of his neck just above the shirt collar because the rest was covered in hair.

'He is a beauty, isn't he?' said the inspector.

'He is absolutely extraordinary, Holmes!' I cried.

'He is a man stuck in the cow pat of life,' said I.

'He is five guineas, Doctor.'

'What was that?' enquired the inspector.

'Nothing to trouble you, Bradstreet. Just a little private business between myself and the sceptical doctor here.' He nodded his head towards the cell. 'This man certainly needs a good grooming. I had an idea that he might, and I took the liberty of bringing the tools with me.' He opened his Gladstone bag as he spoke, and took out, to my astonishment, a cake of Castille soap, some hens eggs, a fine metal comb and a pair of long thin scissors.

'He-he! You are a funny one,' chuckled the inspector.

The last item Sherlock Holmes removed from the Gladstone was a black, cotton apron, which he slung over his head and tied the cords expertly into a bow behind his back. Hullo, thought I – that is not the first time that he has done that. He glanced sideways at me, as if he could read my mind, which he probably could, and caught my eye as I tried to read of some letters embroidered onto the front of the apron. However, for some reason Holmes did not want me to read them and he stooped lower, swerved aside and then turned away from me.

'I say, Holmes, let me see what that fine needlework says on your left boob there...'

'Shut up, Watson. Now, inspector, if you will have the great goodness to open that door very quietly, we will soon make him cut a much more respectable figure.'

'Well, I don't know why I should not,' said the inspector. 'He doesn't look a credit to the Bow Street cells, does he? And you look like you know what you are doing, Mr. Holmes!'

He slipped his key into the lock, and we all very quietly entered the cell. The sleeper half turned, and then settled down once more into a deep slumber. Holmes stooped to the water jug, collected it up into his arms and sprinkled some of the contents over the prisoner's head. The man reacted by elevating himself slowly from the thin bed mattress and making a display of his hair. When he came to his senses, he realised that he was not alone and started to make sudden movements.

'Hold him still, Bradstreet!' The inspector moved behind the seated man and placed his hands firmly upon his shoulders. This put the inspector in full view of the embroidery on the apron; as he read the stitched words his eyes widened, and an appreciative smile wafted across his porky features. Holmes noticed the recognition and made sure that his back was turned *en face* from my view. He flicked a look over his shoulder just to make sure that I was completely obscured.

'Watson – pass me the eggs.'

As I handed Holmes the first egg the prisoner squirmed but when the inspector pressed down harder the man soon gave up the struggle. Holmes cracked three eggs over the prisoner's head and worked them into the hair with his long thin fingers. Inspector Bradstreet and I watched on with keen interest. What was *most* interesting was that even though the prisoner's hair was dampened, we could only see an outline of his skull, and no details of his facial features. His identity was secure; he could have been anyone.

'Now the bar of soap, please, Doctor.' I passed him the cake of globular animal fat, which he rubbed vigorously into the man's orange hair. The reaction was a ball of foam enveloping the man's head Finally, when he sensed that the time was right, Holmes tipped the remains of the water jug over and washed away the foam. The orange tint was washed away and the hair was now black. Before long, all of us could pick out the form and shape of the prisoner's head again but, still, none of his features. However, that was now starting to change right before our eyes as "the great detective" transformed himself before our eyes into "the great hairdresser!" To my astonishment, and much to the surprise of Inspector Bradstreet, Sherlock Holmes flicked the metal comb dexterously through the man's dark locks with his left hand whilst snipping hair off at a rate of knots with his right. As with any demonstration of a highly defined skill, the spectacle for the unsuspecting audience is one of awe and wonder – the way he handled those scissors was a sight to behold! I noticed Bradstreet's jaw drop, and then realised that my own mouth was gaping wide open and, maybe what was only a minute later, Holmes was finished. He still had his back turned towards me when he cast the comb and scissors to one side.

'Let me introduce you,' he shouted, and then jumping aside, arms outstretched in presentation 'to Mr. Neville St. Clair, of Lee, in the county of Kent.'

'Great heaven!' cried the inspector. 'It is indeed the missing man! I know him from the photograph.'

Never in my life have I see such a sight! Bradstreet and I collapsed into spontaneous applause as the man's face, now shorn of its long hair, was revealed by "The Golden Scissors of Soho" himself: Mr. Sherlock Holmes (at least that is what was stitched into the left boob of his apron)! It was at that moment Holmes realised he had accidentally revealed a full view of the embroidery to me. His features dropped from triumph to grimace as he suffered me laughing my socks off at his expense.

'I had no idea that you had won an award for cutting hair, Holmes!' I ejaculated, between guffaws.

'It is not an award, Watson,' he grouched through pinched lips, 'it is a society for the styling, or the "coiffing" of hair. I happen to enjoy it.'

'I happen to enjoy fine lingerie, but I am not known as The Candy Camisole of Camden!' And that sent the inspector and I into a spasm of giggling, and once we started, we couldn't stop.

'For goodness sakes, you two...' Holmes expounded.

I turned my attention to Mr. St. Claire himself. The virtuoso coiff had only fulfilled a proportion of its objective because there, in front of us, sitting on his bed was a pale, sad-faced, refined-looking man, black-haired and smooth-skinned, rubbing his eyes, and

"Would sir like something for the weekend?"

staring about him with sleepy bewilderment and now sporting an amazing new hair style.

'What would one call that particular style, Holmes?' asked I, all poker-faced.

'That is what we call a textured quiff, with faded pompadour.'

Once again, dear reader, I lost my composure and burst into a fit of laughter. Bradstreet joined me for further spasms! Oh, how we laughed at Holmes, now standing languidly with arms folded and fingers tapping impatiently.

'Don't look at me. Look at him!' cried Holmes.

I studied Mr. St. Clair more soberly. Gone was the orange tint which had given him the appearance of being a raving ginger but still there was hair around his eyes and lower forehead. Dammit! There went my wager with Holmes, no better demonstrated by a glance at the great stylist holding up five digits and wearing a silly grin. And then, suddenly, with no pre-meditation, I leapt forwards to confront Mr. St. Clair and clasped his head in my hands. I studied his face. There was the answer! With a rapid, deft flick of my fingers I wrenched the false hair from its spirit gum roots around his eyes and on his forehead, those theatrical falsies being more obvious when up-close.

'Ha-ha!' I cried, holding the sample of hair up triumphantly, 'I knew there was something queer about the facial fuzz, Holmes!'

Mr. St. Clair's face went red and, suddenly realizing his full exposure, he broke into a scream and threw himself down onto his front, burying his face into the pillow. We glanced at one another and waited until his temper had subsided a little. The prisoner then turned on us with the reckless air of a man who abandons himself to his destiny. 'I am undone...' said he resignedly. 'Can anyone tell me what I am charged with?'

'You are charged with making away with Mr. Neville St. Clair!' And then the inspector stopped for some reflection upon what he had just said. 'Erm.... oh, come to think of it, you cannot be charged with that, unless they make case of attempted suicide of it,' said he, with a porcine grin. 'Well, I have been twenty-seven years in the police force, but this really takes the cake.'

'Shouldn't it be a biscuit?' said I.

'Shut up, Watson, and listen to what Mr. St. Clair has to say.'

'If I am Mr. Neville St. Clair,' he mused, 'then it is obvious that no crime has been committed, and that, therefore, I am illegally detained.'

'No crime, but a very great error has been committed,' said Holmes. 'You would have done better to have inveigled your wife... just like the good doctor and I did last night.' And then he tossed me a wink, the rotter!

'It was not the wife I was worried about; it was the children,' groaned the prisoner. 'God help me, I would not have them ashamed of their father. My God, what an exposure! What can I do?'

Sherlock Holmes sat down next to him on the couch and patted him kindly on the shoulder.

'If you leave it to a court of law to clear the matter up,' said he, 'of course you can hardly avoid publicity. On the other hand, if you convince the police authorities that there is no possible case against you, I do not know that there is any reason that the details should find their way into the papers. Inspector Bradstreet would, I am sure, make notes upon anything which you might have to tell us, and submit it to the proper authorities. The case would then never go to court at all.'

'God bless you, Mr. Golden Scissors!' cried the prisoner passionately. 'I would have endured imprisonment, aye, and even execution, rather than have left my miserable secret as a family blot to my children. You are the first who have ever heard my story. My father was a schoolmaster in Chesterfield, where I received an excellent education. I travelled in my youth, took to the stage and finally became a reporter on an evening paper in London. One day my editor wished to have a series of articles upon begging in the metropolis, and I volunteered to supply them. This was the point from which all my adventures started. It was only by trying begging as an amateur that I could get the facts upon which to base my articles. When I had been an actor I had, of course, learned all the secrets of making up, and had been quite famous in the Green Room for my natural skill. I took advantage now of my attainments. At first, I painted my jaw and chin with spirit gum and fixed hair of similar tone to make a scruffy beard. To make myself as pitiable as possible I went with a red head dye in my hair and some appropriately distressed clothing. Then, I took my station at the busiest part of the City, ostensibly as a match-seller, but really as a beggar. For seven hours I plied my trade and when I returned home in the evening I found, to my surprise, that I had received no less than twenty-six shillings and fourpence.

'I wrote my articles and thought little more of the matter until sometime later I backed a horse for a friend that was a "dead certainty" and it went down. Soon I had the bookmaker's bullies set upon me when I couldn't pay up on-the-nail.'

'Ah, we have all been there, haven't we Holmes?'

'Shut up, Watson. Pray, continue with your account, Mr. St. Clair.'

'I was at my wits' end as to where to get the money, but a sudden idea came to me. I begged a fortnight's grace from the bookmaker, asked for a holiday from my employers, and spent the time in begging in the City in my disguise. However, gentlemen, and here is the fascinating nub of my whole story, is that the more hair I stuck to my face, the more sympathy I received and, therefore, the more money was dropped onto me. By the end of the holiday, my head was completely covered in hair and I had not only paid the debt but, also, I had an excess of thirteen pounds. I had the weekends off as well. Well, you can imagine how hard it was to settle down to arduous work at two pounds a six-day week, when I knew that I could earn as much in a day by sticking hair to my face, dying my hair orange and sitting behind a cap on the ground in front of me?

'It was a long fight between my pride and the money, but the latter won at last; I threw up reporting, and sat day after day in the corner which I had first chosen, inspiring pity by my extraordinary head of hair and filling my pockets with coppers. Only one man knew my secret. He was the keeper of a low den in which I used to lodge in Swandam Lane, where I could every morning arrive as decent-looking fellow about to start his working day as an insurance broker in the City of

London and emerge an hour later as a squalid, hirsute and ginger beggar. Once again, in the evenings I was able to transform myself back into a well-dressed man about town. This fellow, a Lascar, was well paid by me for his rooms, so that I knew that my secret was safe in his possession.

'Well, very soon I found that I was saving a considerable sum of money. I do not mean that any beggar in the streets of London could earn seven hundred pounds a year – which is less than my average takings – but I had exceptional advantages in my power of making up, and also in a facility in witty repartee, which improved by practice, and made me quite a recognised character in the City. All day a stream of pennies, varied by silver, poured in upon me, and it was a very bad day upon which I failed to take three pounds.

'As I grew richer, I grew more ambitious. I purchased a house in the country and eventually married, without anyone having any suspicion as to my real occupation. My dear wife knew that I had business in the City, supposedly in the field of insurances, but she knew no detail.

'Last Monday I had finished for the day and was dressing my room above the opium den when I looked out of the window and saw, to my horror and astonishment, that my wife was standing in the street with her eyes fixed full upon me. I gave a cry of surprise, threw up my arms to cover my face, and rushing to my confidant, the Lascar, entreated him to prevent anyone from coming up to me. I heard her voice downstairs, but I knew that she could not ascend. Swiftly, I threw off my clothes, pulled on those of the beggar, and put on my wig and as much of the facial hair disguise as I was able within in such a short period of time. Even a wife's eyes could not pierce so good a disguise as that. But then it occurred to me that there might be a search in the room and that the clothes might betray me. I threw open the window, re-opening by my violence a small cut which I had inflicted upon myself in the bedroom that morning. Then I seized my coat, which was weighted by the coppers which I had just transferred to it from the leather bag in which I carried my takings. I hurled it out of the window, and it disappeared into the Thames. The other clothes would have followed but, at that moment, there was a rush of constables up the stairs, and a few minutes after I found, rather, I confess, to my relief, that instead of being identified as Mr. Neville St. Clair, I was arrested as his murderer.

'I do not know if there is anything else for me to explain. I was determined to preserve my disguise as long as possible, and hence my preference for a very hairy face. Knowing that my wife would be terribly anxious, I slipped off my ring, and confided it to the Lascar at a moment when no constable was watching me, and together with a hurried scrawl, telling her that she had no cause to fear.'

'That note only reached her yesterday,' said Holmes.

'Good God! What a week she must have spent worrying about me!'

Inspector Bradstreet stepped forward. 'The police have watched this Lascar,' said he, 'and I can quite understand that he might find it difficult to post a letter.'

'Why is that, inspector?' enquired Holmes.

'Surely, Holmes,' I interjected, 'being cooped up in that opium den day and night, the man must be off his rocker? I'll bet he doesn't even recognise a post box.'

'That makes sense,' said Holmes, nodding approvingly, 'but is caused Mrs. St. Clair to be extremely concerned. My accomplice and I stayed with her last night. She was restless, hardly slept a wink, but we did our best to comfort her, didn't we Doctor?' And then he tipped me a wink. Was he referring to our late supper or... later on? Was it all a dream... or not? I could not be sure! I glanced back at him and he a smirk that told me he had become my tormentor. How could he read my dreams? Or maybe he couldn't, and that meant that my dream was not a dream at all...

'Well, thank you, gentlemen,' said Mr. St. Clair. 'How can I every thank you enough?'

'It was nothing,' said Holmes. 'This mystery? Whilst it may have presented its puzzles, in the end, the answer to the riddle was a mere trifle for me...' And the great detective waved his hand dismissively, as if he had solved the case in an instant, instead of driving endless miles around the home counties and spent at least one sleepless night wracking his brains and smoking himself to death to find the solution, such was Holmes's vanity. I glanced at Bradstreet, who rolled his eyes towards the ceiling, but I could not look at Mr. St. Clair, so I buried my head into my hands.

'All we ask for, Mr. St. Clair,' I relayed from my hiding place, 'is five guineas to compensate Mr. Holmes's unforeseen out-of-pocket expenses.'

'You shall have it with my blessing!' cried Mr. St. Clair. 'And it won't be in coppers, it will be in gold, I promise you. I have it here, see?'

Neville St. Clair stood up, unfastened his trousers. Instead of letting them drop to the floor, he held onto the waistband with his left hand. 'Would anybody loan me a knife?'

'I am sure The Golden Scissors will lend you his...' I reached for Holmes's delicate shears and handed them to him. Whilst Holmes deflected my ribaldry with a sniff, Mr. St. Clair clipped the inside of his waistband; a few snips later he started to extract gold sovereigns, one after the other.

'And now we have The Golden Trousers!' I quipped.

'Here,' he said to me, offering up five coins, 'this will settle my account with you and go some way to representing my level of gratitude for the service you have offered me and my family.'

At least that was my wager settled. In fact, more than that; I estimated their value to be at least fifty per cent greater than five guineas.

'Your begging career must stop here,' said Bradstreet. 'If the police are to hush this thing up, there must be no more of Hugh Boone.'

'I have sworn it by the most solemn oaths which a man can take.'

'In that case I think that it is probable that no further steps may be taken. But if you are found again, then all must come out. I am sure, Mr. Holmes, that we are very much indebted to you for having cleared the matter up. I wish I knew how you reach your results.'

'I have reached this one,' said my friend, 'by sitting upon five pillows throughout the night, consuming one ounce of shag and...' he paused for the greatest dramatic effect, 'and then putting my body through the most vigorous exercise of the most base but natural kind, wasn't that so Watson?'

What was he saying! 'I...I...I have no idea, Holmes...' I stuttered, and then looked at Bradstreet. 'You see, Inspector, we had a late supper. I fell fast asleep. I was laid out all night. Goodness knows what occurred. I wouldn't have a clue.'

'Ha! Quite so, quite so!' said the heavily-moustachioed policeman. 'You were wise to leave this man's imagination to itself, Doctor, and thus wrap up this confusion for us all.'

The great detective-cum-Golden Scissors coughed a laugh at me and then smiled at us all. He removed his precious apron, collected up his tools of the trade and dropped them into his Gladstone bag.

'I think, Watson, it is time for breakfast. Gentlemen, farewell.'

And with that final address, we left Mr. Neville St. Clair and Inspector Bradstreet to themselves.

* * *

Unfortunately, we never got as far as Baker Street. In fact, we didn't get as far as the front door of Bow Street police station before we were collared once again by the desk sergeant.

'Nah here's someone with sumthin' upstairs. You can 'elp me out with this ...'

Holmes perked up. He stopped and gave the sergeant his full attention.

'In fact, you bein' who you is and all that, is probably the only bloke who can give the answer to this poser.'

A wry smile cracked upon the great detective's features. 'Go on, sergeant. I shall do my best to solve your little problem.'

'Why do coppers never collar gyppos?

'I do not know, sergeant' said Holmes, his body slumping in realisation that he was being fed a crap joke. 'Why do policemen never arrest Romanies?'

'They has crystal balls, so they can see us cummin'! Ha! I'll betcha didn't see *that* cummin', did ya?!'

'Good day to you, sergeant.'

We marched out of the door and had whistled for a constable to extract the dog cart from the pound before the sergeant had stopped laughing. Quite frankly, I was pleased to be alone with the great detective once more. As we stood on Bow Street, I thought about the events of this unique case and how I had been obliged to share our personal space with so many new people for most of the last day or so. Dammit! That word "share" brought back memories of the previous night and revisited my conundrum about last night's erotic *ménage à trois*. Had it all been in my imagination? I resolved to ask Holmes directly, to put him on-the-spot and settle my constitution once and for all. However, as the cart was arriving, Holmes became excited and unusually animated in an aftermath situation. He gathered me in with one arm around my shoulders, up very close, in a manly embrace.

'Ah, what a case that was, Doctor! What a deduction! What an outcome!'

'What a haircut!'

'Indeed, Watson! The Golden Scissors will give you a short back and sides whilst we are waiting for breakfast to be served.'

'Ha! Then it is to Baker Street for one of Mrs. Hudson's hearty breakfasts.'

'To Baker Street? Nonsense Watson, we have five gold sovereigns. Surely we go to Mother Kelly's for breakfast... and tiffin!"

'Yes, I suppose so....'

He gave me an owlish smirk. 'Not very keen, Watson? No *appetite*?'

'No, no, Holmes. That's fine...' I mumbled suspiciously, trying to read the look on his face. What was he implying? I pondered a moment... Where was that terrible urge buried deep in any young man's loins? What about yesterday evening when Mrs. St. Clair pressed her warm body against mine and I resolved to satiate my needs at the earliest chance? Where was that libido? The answer was simple: it was no longer there. So, had my desires been fulfilled yesterday *after* supper?

We climbed up onto the bench, my brain all in a fug, my imagination running wild. Holmes gathered up the reins and passed them to me.

'You drive. After my night's vigil I am drained.' He huddled down into his coat, and then mumbled: 'Literally... drained.'

Drained? My God, it *was* true! It really *did* happen! Memories of last night's *ménage* filled up my imagination once more as I gave the reins a shake. Off we went, clickety-clacking down the cobbles at a leisurely trot, our pony also tired after his night out. I just had to know...

'I say, Holmes, you, being a decent fellow and all that, you will be able to assure me that last night I slept soundly throughout, right up to the very moment you shook me from my slumber, without any sort of interruption whatsoever?'

But there was no answer. I looked over to the great detective, who had fallen to sleep. Bugger! During the journey I cast my mind back once again to the morning and the moment when Holmes woke me up. Yes, it was definitely Holmes waking me up. Yes! And he was fully clothed and our hostess nowhere to be seen. That's right! So, Watson, you are suffering from paranoia; it had all been a dream... Or had it? The nagging doubt festered in my mind as I drove us through Covent Garden to Cambridge Circus, headed up to Old Compton Street, across Berwick, into Carnaby Street and pulled up to a halt in the mews by the rear entrance to Mother Kelly's. By then, I had lost all reason and was desperate to know the truth. I decided to do unto him what he had done to me. I threw down the reins and turned to face him square-on. I grasped a shoulder in each of my hands and shook him hard. I grasped his chin and squeezed hard.

'WAKE UP! WHAT HAPPENED LAST NIGHT? TELL ME! TELL ME!'

Unfortunately, my voice was amplified by the close proximity of the buildings at such an early hour and it attracted the attention of a neighbour nearby; one in particular...

'Hands up, gentlemen!' came the light but authoritative voice from behind me.

I stopped rousting Holmes and turned to look. There, stood by the carriage, was a small chap, maybe only five one or two, completely bald (which made a change from ginger), his skin of a dark hue and dashed with a mean mouth framed by a droopy moustache. He was pointing a silver pistol at us. I didn't know him, but you-know-who certainly did.

'Gripper!' exclaimed Holmes. 'The son of the goddess of predictability.'

'Ha, very amusing, Mr. Holmes. Sticks and stones may break my bones, but an elucidation of Mr. Alexander Pope is flattery.'

Holmes and I gaped at one another and mumbled compliments of appreciation, including my own quip: "no fools rushing in here where angels fear to tread, eh Holmes?" And we laughed.

'You want poetry, gents?' He flicked the barrel of the gun to his right. 'The guv'nor would like some words. With you little turds. See that carriage yonder? Well, don't you ponder. Get yer arses over there. NOW!'

As we dismounted, I had mentioned to Holmes that I was in doubt about the metre but he gestured silence and compliance. We walked over to the smart four-wheeler with Gripper in close attendance, his pistol pointing at our backs all the way. The carriage door swung open and Holmes stepped up. I followed. There was some predictable poetic accompaniment from Gripper, along the lines of: "I'll be watching. No funny business…" That type of thing.

We ended up on the passenger side of the compartment. Our host, Professor Moriarty, was already seated opposite. To see Moriarty was a surprise, but the gentleman seated beside him gave a heart-stopping shock because there, to my astonishment, was a man bound hand and foot and a viciously tight calico gag wound around his mouth. The man sweated terror, with the wide-eyed look of a man about to meet a painful exit of this world. By contrast, Moriarty was calm and debonair, cool as a cucumber.

'Good morning, Sherlock. Please, make yourself comfortable. And welcome aboard, Doctor Watson. How charming it is to see you again.'

'And you too!' I quipped jovially.

Holmes flicked his eyes in my direction. I sensed I had over-emphasised my response.

'Professor,' said Sherlock Holmes quietly, 'why are you interrupting my breakfast?'

'Don't mind Gripper, Sherlock. You know how he is. Loves his pistols.'

'Get on with it,' hissed the great detective impatiently.

'My, how tetchy. You must be hungry!'

'I am, Teddy, I am.'

Suddenly, Moriarty launched himself forwards at Holmes. 'AND SO YOU SHOULD BE!' he snarled. 'Now you know what it feels like!' Then, he relaxed and sat back in his seat. 'And don't call me Teddy. Oh! Where are my manners? May I introduce you to Lord Hamilton...'

Sherlock Holmes pursed his lips. "First Lord of the Admiralty. Good morning, your lordship,' said Holmes, inclining his head. 'I have sympathy for your situation. I am about to be of assistance to you in your release but first we must listen to the rules of the Professor's game and the part I am about to be playing in it.'

A wild-haired Lord Hamilton nodded his head.

'Pray, continue... James.'

'First thing this morning, Lord Hamilton invited me to take possession of these.' Moriarty held up a long, cylindrical collection of papers. 'They are the blueprints for the new battleships and cruisers authorised for construction under the Naval Defence Act of a few weeks ago. Top secret. Top, top secret.'

How fascinating! This morning was turning out to be quite memorable. First, the telephone, and the chance to even touch one, and now a privileged opportunity to preview the designs of our new warships!

'May I?' said I excitedly, pointing at the blueprints.

'No! You may not, Doctor Watson!'

Holmes didn't pass comment. Instead, he drummed his fingers impatiently, looking mighty irritable.

'You have the secret drafts,' he said, 'and you have the First Lord of the Admiralty as your hostage, the two essential ingredients that combine two of the oldest crimes: kidnap and blackmail. My congratulations, James; you are growing up.'

The Professor's face turned dark and angry! He lunged at Holmes, just stopping short this time of dashing his head into the detective's face! He thrust his arm forwards, launching a long quivering finger to stop right under his nose. 'THAT IS ENOUGH, SHERLOCK!' shouted Moriarty, wrangling his mouth to spit the words out. 'That is enough of your preaching! I have had to work hard – very hard – to get ahead in life after what YOU did!'

'I say, it really is very rude to point...' said I, but was ignored by the two gladiators, now locked in conflict.

'James! Your mother was obliged to give me the cream, through no fault of her own.'

Professor Moriarty was an ice-cool operator,
and he took prisoners!

Professor Moriarty went puce and shook with rage. 'DON'T YOU BRING MOTHER INTO THIS!'

Don't bring mother into this? What on Earth was he referring to? I rifled my brains for a clue... then, suddenly, Eureka! it came to me. It must be the moment of that scintillating revelation from Nanny Moriarty – the Professor's mother – on her death-bed.* I had listened to her recounting events of thirty years ago when her husband had absconded at the very moment she gave birth. I learned about how she been forced out onto the street; how, in desperation, she had taken the job as a wet nurse to the Holmes family upon the birth of Sherlock (apparently, Wendy Holmes was not able to express milk) to become Nanny; and, finally, how she had suckled the great detective upon her breast but, being duty-bound to dispense her nourishment to Sherlock as a priority over James, the former had guzzled the gold top and the latter had sucked out the dregs. Consequently, Holmes had turned out large, chubby and rosy whilst Moriarty was a small, thin, puny weakling (and he was probably spotty as well). Nanny had finished off by warning Holmes of the bitter resentment this unavoidable queue-barging had instilled into her son. As a doctor, I knew that the Professor would hold a terrible grudge against the great detective for the rest of his life – and I was correct.

'Stop killing yourself, James!' Holmes advised, wisely. 'You are making a success of your life.' Holmes gestured at the plush interior of the fine carriage. 'Now, to whom would you like me to deliver your demands of blackmail?'

---

*   see *The Oranges of Death!*

'Ah, there is my Sherlock! Always one step ahead...' quipped Moriarty light-heartedly as he retreated into his seat, now all jolly, and pointing his finger in the air (in harmony with his eyebrows). 'Ever since I acquired my two "essential ingredients" as you put it, I have been thinking to myself: I need a messenger-boy, a messenger that has *real* credibility. I have to say, I was a bit stuck for a minute or so and had to postpone my breakfast. *Eggs Rossini*, in there...' He pointed at Mother Kelly's. 'I recommend this dish to you; it is ab-so-lute-ly mouth-watering and fulfilling. I returned to my carriage to ponder when who should turn up? None other than Sherlock Holmes. Now, there's a perfect messenger-boy! The PM will take him seriously.'

'I am not acquainted with Lord Salisbury but go on...'

'It's remarkably simple. You will go to one of those coppers you are acquainted with at Scotland Yard – Gregson? Lestrade? – and ask them to put you in touch with the Prime Minister. You will tell Lord Salisbury everything you have seen here just now. I believe the contract for the construction of these fine ships is about twenty million pounds?' Moriarty glanced at Lord Hamilton, who raised his bound arms and mooed a muffled "Moower!" 'Twenty-five?' Hamilton nodded. 'Please inform his lordship, the PM, that he just acquired me as a partner in this venture, whose consultancy fees are a modest ten per cent. Here is the paperwork for him to sign...' He handed over a bluff envelope to Holmes. '...together with details of the bank in which to deposit the payment. It is in Geneva, of course. Should his lordship think otherwise, he will never see his First Lord of the Admiralty again because he will be tied to an anchor on the bottom of the Thames. Also, these blueprints will be in the clutches of the new Kaiser in Germany, to help him speed up the building of his navy. All very neat and tidy, eh Sherlock?'

'And what if I inform the beaks at Scotland Yard where to find you?'

'Then, the good doctor joins the First Lord of the Admiralty on the bottom of the Thames.'

'Me?' They were looking at me. 'ME?!' How did I get involved in this?

'And why not YOU?'

I thought about it a moment and then nodded. 'I suppose it makes sense...'

'Off you trot, Sherlock. The faster you do it, the quicker it is finished.'

'That applies to most things in life,' said Holmes. Gripper opened the door from outside, the gypsy earwigger that he was, and Holmes disembarked. Just before he set off, my friend leaned in and I could see that there was concern in his eyes. Maybe there was a human side to Sherlock Holmes after all?

'Doctor, try not to annoy the professor with your shaggy dog stories.'

Nope! Holmes was about to depart when I caught his attention. 'Holmes! Just one more thing, I have to know, before you go and maybe never return, so I end up in a watery grave... Last night: did I sleep through peacefully?'

Holmes smiled. 'My dear Watson, when I suggested we breakfast here instead of Baker Street you answered that question yourself.' And with that, the great detective was gone! He left me in a state of deep pontification. I wracked my brains about our conversation of earlier, but I just couldn't remember. *What* had I said?

'*Eggs Rossini*, Doctor Watson?' Professor Moriarty held out his hand in gesture towards the doorway of delights inside Mother Kelly's.

'Goodness me, Professor! You have a reservation for *Eggs Rossini*?!' I replied, in utter astonishment, because this was the hottest ticket in London town and booked up for weeks ahead.

'Indeed, I do, such is my influence. You won't find a better start to the day.'

Indeed so! This was a brand-new concept of Madame's that had been met with an instant accolade of praise from her clientele. 'Why, thank you Professor,' said I effusively, climbing out of the cab as fast as I could. 'If this is what it is like to be a hostage under your wing, I hope that the messenger-boy gets lost!'

The Professor put his hand on my shoulder and stopped me a mo. 'I like the cut of your jib, Doctor,' said he. He looked into my eyes and, oh, how we laughed! I have to say, he seemed to be a thoroughly decent chap. And so, dear reader, my new friend and I bustled our way into London's finest knocking-shop and I forgot all about the conundrum of whether that *ménage à trois* of the previous evening had been real or a dream... forever more.